SMOKING AND QUITTING:
CLEAN AIR FOR ALL

Produced by the CENTRE FOR ADDICTION AND MENTAL HEALTH   Illustrations by JOE WEISSMANN

Smoking and Quitting:
Clean Air for All

Library and Archives Canada Cataloguing in Publication

Smoking and quitting : clean air for all / produced by the Centre for Addiction and Mental Health ; illustrated by Joe Weissman.

Issued also in French under title: Parlons du tabac.
Includes bibliographical references.
For ages 5-10.
Issued also in electronic format.
ISBN 978-1-77052-520-7

1. Smoking--Juvenile fiction. 2. Smoking--Prevention--Juvenile fiction.
3. Picture books for children. I. Weissman, Joe II. Centre for Addiction and Mental Health

PS8600.S66 2011   jC813'.6   C2010-907406-8

ISBN: 978-1-77052-520-7 (PRINT)
ISBN: 978-1-77052-521-4 (PDF)
ISBN: 978-1-77052-522-1 (HTML)
ISBN: 978-1-77052-523-8 (ePUB)

Printed in Canada

This publication may be available in other formats.
For information about alternate formats or other CAMH publications, or to place an order, please contact
Sales and Distribution:
Toll-free: 1 800 661-1111
Toronto: 416 595-6059
E-mail: publications@camh.net

Online store: http://store.camh.net

Website: www.camh.net

Disponible en français sous le titre :
Parlons du tabac : arrêter de fumer pour mieux respirer

This book was produced by:
Development: Susan Rosenstein, CAMH
Writer: Kathy Lowinger
Illustrator: Joe Weissmann, working in watercolours
Editorial: Jacquelyn Waller-Vintar and Nick Gamble, CAMH
Design: Eva Katz, CAMH
Print production: Christine Harris, CAMH

Production of this document has been made possible through a financial contribution from Health Canada.
The views expressed herein do not necessarily represent the views of Health Canada.

4166 / 01-2011 / P5609

About the many people who worked on this book

We would like to thank the CAMH (Centre for Addiction and Mental Health) project team: Susan Rosenstein, MA, publishing developer and project manager, publications unit of the Policy, Education and Health Promotion Department; Stephanie Cohen, MSW, RSW, therapist II, Nicotine Dependence Clinic; Rosa Dragonetti, MSc, Nicotine Dependence Clinic; Sherri Mackay, PhD, CPsych, head, TAPP-C Program, in Child, Youth and Family Program; Irfan Mian, MD, FRCPC, clinical head, Mood and Anxiety Disorders Service and the Children's Psychotic Disorders Service, Child, Youth and Family Program, and assistant professor, University of Toronto; Roberta Ferrence, PhD, senior scientist, Social and Epidemiological Research Department, executive director, The Ontario Tobacco Research Unit, University of Toronto; Marilyn Herie, PhD, RSW, advanced practice clinician, director, TEACH Project; Krystyna Ross, publisher and manager, Publication Services within Policy, Education and Health Promotion; Peter L. Selby, MBBS, CCFP, MHSc, FASAM, clinical director, Addictions Program, clinical head, Nicotine Dependence Clinic at CAMH, associate professor departments of Family and Community Medicine, Psychiatry, and the Dalla Lana School of Public Health, University of Toronto, principal investigator with The Ontario Tobacco Research Unit; Cindy Smythe, MA, research associate, Social and Epidemiological Research Department.

We have special thanks for the following professionals from across Canada who reviewed early versions of this book and provided invaluable insight and feedback and/or consulted on specific issues: Kim Alford, BS, CHES, tobacco treatment specialist, Sault Ste. Marie Tribe of Chippewa Indians, Sault Ste. Marie, Michigan; Cindy Baker-Barill, RN, BNSc, Central East tobacco control network area planner, Simcoe Muskoka District Health Unit; Sandy Bollenbach, Grade 1 teacher, Portage Trail Jr. Community School, Toronto, ON; Donna Pasiechnik, manager, Tobacco Control, Media and Government Relations, Canadian Cancer Society, Regina, SK; Rhae Ann Bromley, director of communications, Heart and Stroke Foundation of Saskatchewan, Moose Jaw, SK; Jeff D'Hondt, manager, Aboriginal Services, CAMH; John Hoysted, RSW, social worker, Merrickville and District and Smiths Falls Community Health Centre, ON; Dan Ingram, area manager, Heart and Stroke Foundation of Ontario, Sault Ste. Marie, ON; Jennifer McFarlane, health promotion planner, Alcohol and Substance Misuse, Thunder Bay District Health Unit, Thunder Bay, ON; Angela McKercher-Mortimer, BCW, CYW, youth development specialist with Kingston, Frontenac and Lennox & Addington Public Health, Kingston, ON; Karen McLean, tobacco control consultant, Toronto, ON; Ron Pohar, BSc PHARM, pharmacist, Edmonton, AB; Robin Reese, tobacco control specialist, Heart and Stroke Foundation of Ontario, Toronto, ON; Cristine Rego, MSW, RSW, provincial aboriginal training consultant, CAMH Aboriginal Services, Sudbury, ON; Scott M. Sellick, PhD, CPsych, director of Supportive Care, Thunder Bay Regional Health Sciences Centre, Thunder Bay, ON; David Tantalo, BASc, CPHI(C), MBA, co-ordinator of environmental health, Renfrew County and District Health Unit, Pembroke, ON; Cathy Thompson, program consultant, CAMH; and Cheryl Vrkljan, MSc, program consultant, CAMH, Hamilton, ON.

Parents with knowledge of tobacco use and their children also reviewed the book and provided additional insight.

Eee-ooo eee-ooo eee-ooo! We could hear the fire truck. Everyone from our building gathered on the sidewalk while the firefighters did their work. Soon the fire was out. One of the firefighters made an announcement.

"Everyone can go back inside now, folks. You were all very lucky. There's been little damage done."

"What happened? How did the fire start?" asked Mrs. Charles.

The firefighter held up a small lighter. "It looks like this was the culprit. We found it in the laundry room by a stack of newspapers. Do any of you smoke?"

4

Mom looked guilty. My sister, Meg, stared at her shoes. Eli Solomon nodded slowly. Mr. Becker stubbed a cigarette out under his foot.

"It could have been any of you, even these young fellows." The firefighter gestured toward the Solomon twins. They can get into all kinds of mischief.

"But they're so young, they don't know any better," said their dad, Eli.

"Lighters and matches can tempt children. Cigarette smoking is one of the main causes of house fires. Some people even fall asleep while they're smoking," said the firefighter.

Mrs. Charles coughed. "I guess anyone could have caused this."

That was a scary thought. I took my sister's hand. "Our homes could have burned down."

"It's okay, Daniel," Meg said. But I could tell by her face that things weren't okay at all.

5

The next day, my neighbour Trev and I were tossing a ball when the visiting nurse, Lorraine, came to check on Mrs. Charles. Mrs. Charles used to smoke and now she has trouble breathing. She has to use oxygen. When we told Nurse Lorraine what had happened the night before, she looked serious. "Fire's not the only dangerous thing about smoking. Smoking can make you very sick. You can get infections easier, and diseases too."

Mrs. Charles coughed. Nurse Lorraine shook her head sadly. "Wow, you were lucky. A spark could have made the oxygen tank explode! This could have been far worse. I'm happy everyone is safe."

Just then Mr. Becker came home with Marmalade in his cat carrier. Mr. Becker looked very worried.

"Is something wrong with Marmalade, Mr. Becker?" I asked. Marmalade gave a sad meow.

"The vet says that he's sick because of my smoking. The smoke is hurting his lungs. I would never want to hurt Marmalade. He's a fine cat. I've got to do something about my smoking."

We were about to go in when we heard a bike bell ringing. Zack, our upstairs neighbour, hopped off his bike.

"Were you training for the big race?" I asked as Kate rode up, panting.

"I just can't improve my time," she said. "The race is at the end of the summer and I'll never be ready."

"I wish you'd quit smoking," said Zack. "I'm sure you could breathe better then. Besides, I hate the smell of cigarettes on your hair and clothes."

Kate turned red and marched into the building. I don't think she liked being reminded how bad smoking was for her—and for others.

That evening after dinner, while Meg and I cleaned up, Mom said she was going to take Oscar out for a walk.

"But it's pouring, Mom. Oscar hates the rain."

"That makes two of us," Mom laughed, but she went anyway.

Meg and I exchanged looks.

"She thinks we don't know she still smokes," said Meg. "Maybe she's ashamed. Remember when she tried to quit and she said it just made her cough more?"

"And she said that it made her grumpy. You know, she only smokes outside now. I guess she's trying to protect us from breathing in the smoke."

"I think so too. But in school I learned that smoking outside helps, but there are still harmful cigarette chemicals left in the house from when she smoked inside. I wish she'd stop," said Meg. "I worked out how much money cigarettes cost. She keeps complaining that she needs a new computer, but if she quits she can buy one with the money she saves."

The next day in school we had current events. It was Trev's turn to present the news. He had picked a story about the danger of second-hand smoke in cars. During the question period I asked about something that had been puzzling me. "If people know that it's so bad for them, why do they smoke?"

"It's a habit, isn't it Mrs. Whitefish?" asked Trev.

Mrs. Whitefish explained. "It's more than a habit. It's an addiction. This means that the body and the brain become so used to a drug that it becomes very difficult to live without." That brought lots more questions from the class.

"Does that mean you can't quit?"

"No. You can quit! But the best thing is never to start."

"Is it too late for my parents? Are they going to get sick from smoking?" Trev looked worried.

"Well, the sooner someone quits the better it is. The body starts to repair itself within hours. And the longer you don't smoke, the better it is too."

I thought about Mr. Becker and poor Marmalade. "Are you ever too old to quit?"

"No. Quitting at any age is better than not stopping at all. It's hard to quit for many people, but it's possible. Some people are able to quit the first time they try. It takes others several times before they are successful. But even though it's hard, it's never too late to quit."

When I opened the door to our apartment building after school, the smell
of cigarette smoke hit me like never before. And that's when I had an idea.

"We need to call a special meeting for everyone who lives here," I said to Trev.

"Like when the roof had to be fixed, and the time we talked about recycling?"

"This time, the meeting will be about smoking. I think we should all be living in a smoke-free building!"

I could see that Trev liked the idea. We made a sign. "Meeting on the lawn. Today 6:00 p.m. Free lemonade."

Everybody came: Eli Solomon and the twins, Mr. Becker, Trev's folks, Mrs. Charles, Zack and Kate, and my mom and my sister Meg. Oscar wagged hello to everybody. Marmalade watched from the window.

Trev and I were nervous about talking to so many grown-ups so we tossed a coin to decide who would start.

I cleared my throat. "We are tired of living in a smoky building. We don't want to worry about fires or getting sick. And we don't want you to get sick." Oscar barked. "And we don't want our pets to get sick either. By the end of summer we want the whole building to be smoke free!"

The adults looked at one another.

"I'm in," said Eli.

"Me too," said Kate.

"We're quitting!" said Trev's mom and dad together.

Mr. Becker raised his glass of lemonade. "I'm going to give it a try for me and for Marmalade—and for all of you."

Mom didn't say anything. After all, her smoking was supposed to be a secret. "What about it, Mom?" asked Meg.

Mom blushed, but she said, "I'm quitting too." Oscar wagged his tail.

That's how things got started. Everybody had a plan to keep their minds off smoking.

Kate took up yoga.

Eli Solomon went to the doctor and she prescribed medicine for him to take.

Trev's parents used nicotine gum and did puzzles during times they used to smoke cigarettes.

Mr. Becker sucked on lollipops and ate carrot sticks.

Mom just crumpled up her cigarette package and threw it away. "I'm just going to quit on my own, starting right now!" she announced.

The first month went by. We soon learned that quitting was different for everybody. Kate had a hard time; she slipped up and had a cigarette, but then she called Eli Solomon to help her get back on track. Mr. Becker hadn't had a cigarette after the first week. "It's a snap," he announced. "I don't know why I didn't quit years ago."

But for Mom, it wasn't so easy. I know she tried, but it was really hard for her. She would go for a day or two without having a cigarette and then she started smoking again. She didn't even bother to pretend she was walking Oscar.

I was discouraged. On a rainy Saturday morning, Zack found me crying in the stairway. "Why do people smoke when they know it will hurt them or others?" I wiped my eyes.

Zack sat down beside me. "Daniel, I don't think there's a simple reason. Nobody starts to smoke thinking that they'll get addicted."

"Is it just that Mom doesn't have the willpower? Can't she just stick to her decision? Doesn't she care about us?"

"Of course she cares! She's trying, and it takes time for some people to be successful."

It was time for Meg and me to walk Oscar, so we took him to the schoolyard. Some of Meg's friends were there. One of them pulled out a pack of cigarettes and handed them around.

"No, thanks," I said.

The girl held the pack out to Meg. "What's the matter, are you a baby?" she said when Meg shook her head.

Meg looked at me and then turned to her friends. "Smoking is stupid. Why would I want to do something that's so bad for me?" I was really proud of her.

The summer wore on and Mom tried to quit again and again. We all cheered up when Grandma came for a visit. She was excited to hear about Mom's efforts and our plan to make our building smoke free.

While Mom was fixing lunch, Grandma and I curled up on the couch. "Grandma, Mom's trying hard to quit smoking. Do you think it's my fault that she smokes? If I listened better maybe she wouldn't feel like she needs a cigarette."

"It is not your fault, and it isn't your responsibility."

"I wish I could help her."

"You are helping her, Daniel."

"How?" I was doubtful.

"Well, you let her know you love her, no matter what. It's so great that you're talking to your mom about your feelings and concerns. Talking about things that worry you is important. And I like the way you celebrate her successes."

I knew she meant the stars Meg and I put on the calendar for every one of Mom's smoke-free days. Talking with Grandma made me feel better.

The end of summer finally came. It was the day of the bike race. We all cheered Zack and Kate on. They rode their best times ever. And that night, we had a party. We had a lot to celebrate. Our building was almost smoke-free! Mr. Becker didn't have to have a lollipop in his mouth anymore. Eli Solomon had taken up jogging.

Trev's folks were slicing a watermelon. My mom raised a glass of lemonade. "Here's to all of us and our efforts to quit smoking! Clean air for all!"

I knew that for Mom the challenge to stop smoking wasn't over, but she was really trying. I knew she would succeed. And I knew that the best advice for me was to never start smoking in the first place!

INFORMATION FOR ADULTS

Ways to use this book

This book is meant as an educational resource and, more importantly, as a way to open a dialogue about smoking between teachers, parents, other caregivers, family members and children. Anti-smoking messages to children in schools and via media outlets are important, but can cause confusion and concern for kids, especially if parents, caregivers, other family members and people they admire smoke. This book is intended to address those concerns as well as to give children some strategies for protecting themselves from second-hand smoke.

Some suggested uses of the book include:
- integrating the book into elementary school curricula through a classroom or library reading circle, followed by facilitated discussion with students
- as a starting point for a collaborative school group project about smoking risks, consequences and prevention strategies for students
- for parents, caregivers or other family members to read and discuss with children
- for a child to read on her or his own, then discuss
- for adults or older children to read independently.

Note that the scenarios and characters in the story may not be 100 per cent realistic—the intent of the book is to share, in a clear and straightforward way, the risks of smoking and second-hand smoke, what can happen when a person smokes, how to protect yourself and others from second-hand smoke, ways of quitting, and how to support family members and others who want to quit.

The book is also a tool for talking to kids about smoking when a "teachable moment" presents itself. This might be when a child asks a question or makes a comment about smoking, notices smoking-related litter (e.g., cigarette butts or packaging), or sees a character smoking in a movie. The important thing is to start the conversation—smoking is the leading preventable cause of death worldwide, and kids have many, often unexpressed, questions.

Tobacco use and your family

Parents want their children to be healthy. When asked, most parents who smoke do not want their children to smoke. Unfortunately, however, children are more likely to become smokers if their parents smoke, if anyone in their home smokes, or if the people in their peer group smoke. That's why it's so important for parents to know how they can increase the likelihood that children won't smoke. It's crucial for family members to know how they can protect their children from second-hand smoke and how they can help them (and themselves) quit if they already smoke.

This book provides helpful and easy-to-understand answers to children's common questions when a parent smokes cigarettes, and it offers the parent, grandparent, teacher, mental health or addiction professional, or other concerned adult a tool to aid in talking with children about smoking. Encouraging children to start talking about family issues related to smoking is important. Even if you are still smoking yourself, there are many things you can do to minimize the risks to your children. Even if you smoke and do not intend to quit, this book can be a useful way to open the door to an ongoing conversation about your child's concerns, questions and ideas. This book will help you talk to your kids about this difficult topic with ease, especially if you feel shame or guilt about your own smoking.

Kids' commonly asked questions

If everyone knows that smoking is bad for your health, why do people do it?
Even with Canadian advertising bans on tobacco products, cigarette smoking is often still shown in films, including movies and cartoons aimed at children. Cigarettes are among the most sophisticated drug-delivery devices ever invented, meaning that

children and teens who experiment with smoking are more likely to become dependent on smoking than on any other drug they might try.

Why is it so hard for some people to quit smoking?

The nicotine in cigarettes changes the brain's internal reward system, and that change is what causes dependence. Nicotine acts on the same part of the brain as other drugs of dependence, such as cocaine and heroin. Once the drug nicotine has "hijacked" the brain, a person becomes addicted and needs to smoke to avoid unpleasant withdrawal symptoms. Another reason why it is hard for many people to quit is the constant repetition ("hand-to-mouth") behaviour of regular smoking. It's also hard to quit when cigarettes are widely available, and when people are around others who are smoking. Smoking becomes associated with other pleasurable activities, like going for a walk, having a meal, socializing with friends, and so on. When a person tries to quit, all of these activities become constant reminders or "triggers" to smoke.

Are my parents going to get sick and die from smoking?

Tobacco use seems harmless at first because it takes many years for a person to get sick from smoking. But the truth is that smoking is associated with almost every disease imaginable, including emphysema, heart disease, cancer (including breast cancer), diabetes, mental health problems such as depression, and other addictions. About half of the people who keep smoking will die from a disease caused by smoking, so it is a big risk. The good news is that it is never too late to quit smoking, and it is the single most important thing a person can do to stay healthy. Scientists have developed many effective medications to help people quit, and counselling can make a person's attempt to quit even more likely to be successful. At the end of this section are some suggestions for where to get help with quitting smoking.

If there is smoking around me, how can I protect myself and others?

Second-hand smoke is even more toxic than the smoke inhaled directly from a cigarette, since the tobacco burns at a lower temperature. That lower temperature means more tar and carbon monoxide in the air. The best thing is to make your house and car smoke free. If you are a smoker, then smoking outside can keep others (including pets) from getting sick because of second-hand smoke.

These questions represent real concerns from children. Anti-smoking campaigns have successfully conveyed the message that tobacco use is dangerous; cigarettes are the only legal consumer product that kills approximately 50 per cent of customers when used as intended. The bottom line is that smoking can hurt you. Quitting reduces the harm.

It's important to talk about smoking

Kids often worry when they see family members they love doing something dangerous to their health that may even kill them. Most children know the basic fact that smoking is bad for your health. Many children know this at a young age. They don't understand why people do something they know is bad for them. Many children also know that second-hand smoke is bad for them and they worry about how to protect themselves. Children shouldn't have to protect themselves. That's the job of parents and caregivers.

- **Serious health problems**. Issues related to tobacco use are complex and the resulting health problems are serious. Cigarette smoke is the leading cause of preventable death. Many children are still exposed to second-hand smoke in their homes and in their communities at the entrances to buildings, on sidewalks, in parks, and inside cars. This is because smoke-free laws do not cover every situation, and not everyone obeys them. Even with current restrictions, second-hand smoke continues to harm people of all ages: unborn babies, infants, children, teens, adults and seniors.

- **Second-hand smoke and residue**. Research has shown that the health issues for children exposed to second-hand smoke are even more serious than we knew before. There are many harmful chemicals in second-hand smoke: residues from smoke contain heavy metals and carcinogens, and these can be found in homes and vehicles where people smoke. Second-hand smoke can be more harmful than inhaled smoke. There can be huge exposure even when the actual "smoke" is not present. The micro-particles of tobacco smoke cling to walls, upholstery and carpeting and continue to "off-gas" even after the cigarette is extinguished. In infants and children, second-hand smoke causes sudden infant death syndrome (SIDS), asthma and other respiratory diseases, ear infections and possibly brain tumours. It even causes cancer and breathing problems in family pets.

- **Influence of parental smoking on children's attitudes about smoking**. Children have an increased likelihood of smoking if their parents smoke. Some studies have even found that having older siblings who smoke can affect younger siblings' use of tobacco. On the other hand, they are less likely to smoke if they know their parents disapprove of smoking and if they don't allow smoking in the home.

- **Increased risk of house fires**. House fires are another serious risk that children are exposed to when someone in the family smokes indoors. Cigarettes are the number one cause of fire-related death in Canada. Raising awareness of this preventable hazard will help reduce the risk and save lives.

- **Benefits of quitting**. It's never too late to quit smoking. In fact, there are major benefits to quitting at any age. It may take several attempts to succeed, so it is important to view quitting as a process, rather than as a single event. The body starts to repair itself within hours of stopping smoking. The longer you stay smoke free, the greater the health benefits. It's important for children to see the people they love trying to be healthy.

Aboriginal Peoples may have their own teachings about tobacco. Elders and others who maintain traditional practices are a good resource for learning more about the spiritual and ceremonial uses of tobacco in many Aboriginal families, communities, Nations or organizations.

Children shouldn't have to protect themselves. That's the job of parents and caregivers. Encouraging children to talk to you and others about smoking and to acknowledge and respond to their concerns are some of the most important things you can do for them.

Where you can get help

Talk to your doctor about how to quit smoking.

Talk to your pharmacist, nurse, health care professional or local health unit.

Visit www.gosmokefree.gc.ca for extensive information on tobacco use and quitting from Health Canada.

Visit www.camh.net for resources about tobacco use.

Visit www.cancer.ca/smokershelplines or call the Canadian Cancer Society at 1 888 939-3333 to get a toll-free number for a smokers' helpline in your province or territory.

Visit www.tobaccowise.com to learn more about the Aboriginal Tobacco Program (ATP) that works with Aboriginal communities to decrease and prevent the misuse of tobacco.